First paperback edition 1994
Reprinted 1995, 1996, 1997, 1999, 2003, 2005

First published 1988 in hardback by A&C Black Publishers Ltd
37 Soho Square, London, W1D 3QZ
www.acblack.com

ISBN 0-7136-4082-0

A CIP catalogue record for this book is available from the British Library

Acknowledgements
The author and publisher would like to thank all the staff and pupils at Barham
School, especially Dorothy, Benn and Winmarie. They would also like to thank
Sanjay and his family for their help and hospitality.

A & C Black uses paper produced with elemental chlorine-free pulp, harvested from
managed, sustainable forests.

Filmset by August Filmsetting, Haydock, St Helens
Printed in China by Imago

Diwali

Chris Deshpande

Photographs by Prodeepta Das

A & C Black · London

Diwali is almost here. It's the Hindu Festival of Light so the streets are all decorated and lit up. Everyone is getting ready to celebrate.

At home, people are lighting divas (lamps).

At school, children are making divas to light up the classroom.

Hindus all over the world light divas to celebrate the time when King Rama returned to his kingdom of Ayodhya.

Parul is painting her diva on the window.

Deepa and Rahim enjoyed listening to the story of Diwali. It tells how Rama defeated his evil enemy, Ravana.

They decided to make a big picture of Rama, so Rahim lay on the floor and Deepa drew around him.

Here is their picture.

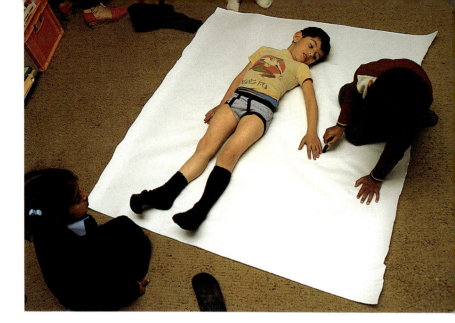

To make the model of Ravana, Tara and her friends drew around Les, the school caretaker. Then they stuffed the model with scrunched up newspaper.

Ravana has many heads. Can you count how many he has?

If you don't know the story of Diwali, why not ask someone to tell it to you?

Near to Sanjay's home is
a shop which sells
Diwali cards. Sanjay is
choosing cards to send
to his friends.

Sapphire and Andrew have decided to make their
own cards to send to their mums and dads.
They think it's more fun.

Sanjay has found some pretty rangoli patterns in the shop. They are made with brightly coloured powders and put on the doorstep to welcome visitors to the house.

Sanjay thinks they are great!

Sheetal thought it would be a good idea to welcome her friends into the classroom. She didn't have any coloured powder, so she decided to chalk a rangoli pattern on the doorstep instead.

Diwali is a very happy time when people get
dressed up and go to parties and dances.

Tara and her friends are getting ready for their
school's Festival of Light.

Everyone has put on their new clothes.
Nilesh is painting a mendhi pattern on Tara's
hand. Mendhi is made from the powdered leaves
of the henna plant which is mixed with water.

Shannon is decorating his headteacher's hand.

And they've made a picture with lots of different mendhi patterns.

At last it's Diwali and everybody is busy preparing food.

Some food will be needed for the parties. One of the mums comes into school to help the children with their cooking.

Some food is cooked and taken to the mandir (temple). It is offered to the gods for their blessing.

After the food has been blessed, it is shared amongst the people at the mandir. Everyone has a little bit to take home.

Sanjay's mum is busy cooking. Sanjay and his family have invited some friends to their house to join in their Diwali celebrations.

Here is Sanjay's mum making dhokla, and these are the ingredients which she needs.

Sanjay likes to help his mum.
He is garnishing the dhokla. He likes to eat
it with coconut flakes sprinkled on the top.

Sanjay's mum and dad have their own family shrine at home. The family do their puja (prayers) in front of the shrine every day. On their shrine, they have pictures of the gods which they pray to.

In the evening when all the guests have arrived, Sanjay and his family and friends perform the Sacred Fire Ceremony and sing the aarti prayers.

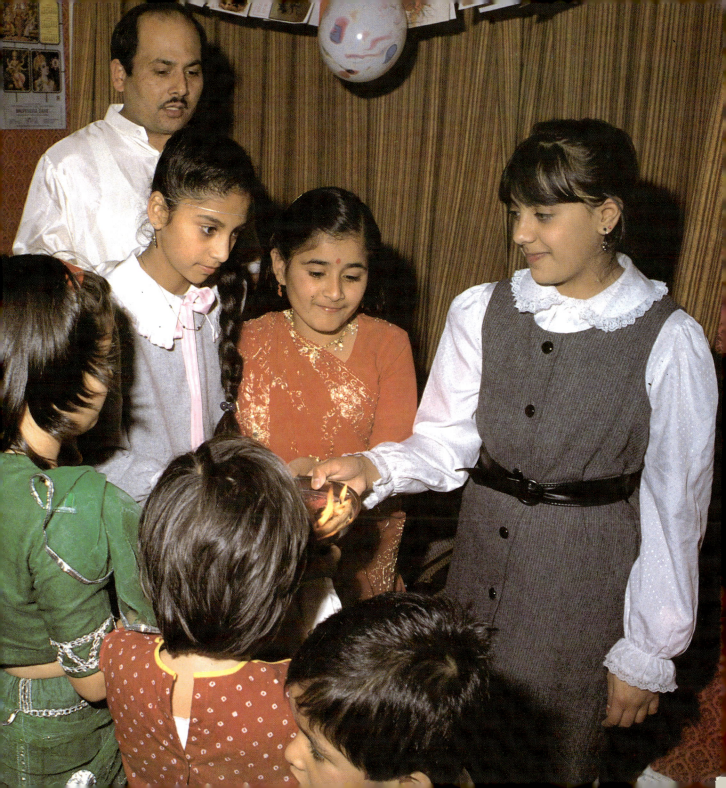

When the aarti is over, the children sit down
to eat all the wonderful things which Sanjay's
mum has cooked.

Sanjay and Tara are
lucky because they also
have Diwali parties at
school.

All the children bring in
food for the parties and
some of the mums and
dads come too.

As well as the parties, there are lots of dances around Diwali time.

Garba and dandia raas are dances which are great fun to do.

To dance the dandia raas, everyone has dandia (sticks) and they dance around their partners and tap their sticks together.

The music starts quite slowly and then gets faster and faster.

Although it's great fun, you have to be careful that you don't hit your partner's fingers instead of the sticks!

Here's a picture of the dancers with their sticks.

Last of all, there's a big fireworks party at school.
The fireworks are lit to celebrate Rama's victory
over Ravana. There's a huge bonfire, too.

Lots of people who live near the school come to watch.

There are all kinds of fireworks whizzing and banging. Sanjay and Tara think it's a wonderful way to end Diwali and they're looking forward to next year.

More about Diwali

Diwali is a celebration of the victory of good over evil. It also marks the end of the year. A very important part of Diwali, which we have not dealt with in the book, is the Lakshmi puja. Lakshmi is the goddess of well-being and plays a very significant part in the religious aspect of Diwali.

The Ramayana is the story most commonly connected with Diwali, although there are many others. It's a very beautiful and exciting story which children enjoy hearing, so it is well worth reading the full story to them.

Here is a *very* brief outline of the story. Prince Rama and his wife, Sita, have been banished from their home in Ayodhya by their father, the King. Rama's brother, Lakshman, goes with them. They are banished for fourteen years.

After many happy years in the forest, Sita is kidnapped by the ten-headed demon Ravana. Ravana takes her to his island of Lanka. With the help of Hanuman, the monkey general, Rama rescues Sita and kills Ravana in battle.

The people of Ayodhya light divas to guide Rama and Sita back from the forest to Ayodhya. On his return, Rama is crowned King.

24

You may not have heard some of the words in this book. This is how they are usually pronounced.

Rama	*Raam (like calm)*
Sita	*Seeta*
Lakshman	*Lucksh-mun*
Ravana	*Raavan*
Hanuman	*Hanumaan*
Puja	*Pooja*
Diva	*Deeva*
Lakshmi	*Lucksh-mee*

Things to do

1. Try to find out about these characters and what they did in the Ramayana:

Shoorpanakha having her nose cut off.

Hanuman setting fire to Lanka.
The golden deer.

2. Find out how to make dhokla; or ask your friends what they like to eat at festivals or at special times. You could make a recipe book and then try all the different foods.

3. Make face masks of all the main characters in the Ramayana and then act out the story.

4. Learn how to do the dandia raas or garba, they are easy. Perhaps you can get some dandia and then decorate them.

5. Divas are fun to make. Make them out of clay or Plasticine.

6. Find out all you can about Lakshmi. Why is she important?

7. Henna is a plant; find out where it grows and what it looks like. Muslims also use henna; try to find out when and how it is used.

8. Diwali is a festival of light. There are many other festivals around the world in which light plays an important part. How many can you find? Perhaps you can make a book called 'Festivals of Light'.

9. Diwali is also an important celebration time for Sikhs. At this time of year, Guru HarGobind Singh and 52 Hindu rajas were released from prison. Find out more about this story.